COMMITMENT

a

Romantic Novel

by

Vince D'Angelo

Published by Simon Publishing LLC
Naples, Florida

Printed by Ingram Spark
United States of America

Landrock County, New York. Circa 2000

The three were standing in the foyer of the modest home.

"Boyd Contracting, eh?" spoke the balding, middle-aged man as he looked up from the business card at the younger man whose jeans, plaid shirt, and tussled brown hair was covered with specks of sawdust.

"You come highly recommended, Mr. Boyd," declared David Sarnoff, the homeowner, as he put the card in a pocket of his vest. His apron-clad wife Rachel, holding a napkin, looked alternately at the two men.

"Always nice to hear," said Michael Boyd with an appreciative smile. I have done quite a bit of work in this development." He glanced at the napkin. "I didn't mean to interrupt your dinner. I happened to be passing by from a job I'll be finishing in about a week. After that I can get yours started. That is, if you want me to do the work." He paused. "I work on a time and material basis. My hourly rate is—"

"Not a problem, Mr. Boyd. You can start whenever you're available. The house isn't going anywhere and neither are we," said the homeowner with a gurgling chuckle. His wife nodded in approval as she regarded the smiley-eyed contractor.

Rachel Sarnoff was at the kitchen sink doing the breakfast dishes. Hearing a car door slam, she

1

looked out through the kitchen window. A large white, van was stopped in the driveway. She caught a glimpse of someone walking toward the front entrance. She wiped her hands on her apron, removed it and placed it on a nearby kitchen stool. As she walked to the front door, her hands smoothed down her plain, gray-green housedress and ran her fingers through her short, auburn hair.

"Coming, coming," she called out to the sound of the chimes. She opened the door without unlatching the safety chain and peered out.

"Hello Mrs. Sarnoff, it's Michael Boyd," said a cheerful voice.

"Oh, yes, of course," said the woman as she unhooked the chain.

"You were expecting me, weren't you?" Boyd wiped his shoes on the entrance mat. "I spoke with Mr. Sarnoff two nights ago to say I'd be here this morning."

"Yes, yes. He told me, but I didn't see any name on the truck."

"That's because I don't have a name on it," said Boyd with a small chuckle in his voice. "Sorry if I took you by surprise—"

"Not such a problem," said the woman as she unlatched the safety-chain and held the door open.

Boyd, carrying a clipboard, stepped inside. "Just gonna take some measurements and make a materials list this morning Then I'll be gone until after lunch and I'll be back later with some material."

"Fine. I'm not going anywhere."

Boyd waited for her to lead him to the room where the work was to take place. She seemed momentarily distracted.

"Come, I'll show you." She closed the door and brushed quickly by Boyd. While following her, he plucked a measuring tape from his work belt. He noticed, the plain dress and the matronly brown shoes she wore, were much the same as those worn by the other women in the development. "I'll try to stay out of your way much as I can, Mrs. Sarnoff. I understand we're to make one of the bedrooms into a den."

"Abigail's room. She left for college. She's getting married and won't be coming back home," said the woman sullenly. "My son Aaron, they're twins, left too. He'll be living back here after college…I suppose."

Boyd could see it was not a happy time for her, both kids leaving home at the same time. And the reason for her down demeanor.

"I have notes on what's to be done that I made after I spoke to Mr. Sarnoff over the phone," he said as he entered the bedroom. He turned looking at each of the walls. Then, talking as if to himself, "Let's see, on the large far wall—" He glanced over at Mrs. Sarnoff who was standing in the doorway.

"Do you have any questions?" she said as if in explanation for still being there.

"No, I'm fine, thanks."

She turned and walked away. He watched her for a moment, and then turned all around to familiarize himself with the style and character he needed to replicate. He saw that the interior of the house was much the same as the others he had worked on in the development: one-floor ranch-style houses built in the same year, all furnished in much the same style. And occupied by similarly dressed occupants. The men wore black clothes and small skullcaps. The women all wore the same plain dresses and hefty shoes that weren't in keeping with the fashions of the time.

Some time back he had commented about it to an electrician who'd also been working in the development. The man told him the homeowners were known as Reform Jews who chose to live in the clan-like community surrounding a Synagogue. Boyd admired their adherence to those disciplines, comparing them to the people of his own Catholic faith who were casual in dress, demeanor and church attendance.

After making out his materials list he walked to the front door. "Be back in a few hours," he called out. "I'll let myself out."

"Fine," came a reply from somewhere in the house.

On the way back from the supply yard he stopped at a sandwich shop. While having lunch he was thinking that there was something different about Mrs. Sarnoff from the other women in the development. It may just be she's younger, prettier and has a slight accent.

When he returned, Rachel Sarnoff, responding to the sounding of the chimes, again peered through the small, chained, opening before unlatching it.

"I need the garage door to be opened, Mrs. Sarnoff. I have material to put in there. Hopefully there's enough room."

"There's more room in the unfinished part of the basement if you need, Mr. Boyd."

The garage door rose. Mrs. Sarnoff was standing inside next to a black Mercedes wearing a dress with a floral design. She also had on slightly higher-heeled, more fashionable shoes. Her wavy auburn hair looked brushed and shiny and was wearing some makeup. He assumed she was going out shopping.

"Hope I didn't hold you up, Mrs. Sarnoff."

"No, it's okay."

He pulled out the lengths of moldings protruding through the rear doors of his van, and carried them into the garage as she watched. He put the material along the other car space, which was empty.

"I left enough room for Mr. Sarnoff's car," he said as he walked past Mrs. Sarnoff. "It'll only be there, for a short while."

She walked over to a wall and pushed the garage door button. As the large door rumbled down, he followed her through the basement entry door. "It's starting to get cold," he said, to make a little small talk. She didn't comment.

When he stopped working for the day he walked over and stood in the archway leading to the kitchen. Rachel Sarnoff was standing at the sink counter with her back to him. "I don't want to continue pulling things apart at this late hour, Mrs. Sarnoff, so I'll be leaving."

She turned facing him. "Rachel, call me Rachel. You can work as late as you wish. I'm not going anywhere or expecting anyone."

"Thanks…Rachel." He felt a little uncomfortable calling a client by a first name. "I'll be back at eight thirty tomorrow morning if it's okay with you."

"Fine, Mr. Boyd"

He waited a moment because she looked as though she wanted to say something more.

"I'll let myself out."

As he drove away he wondered about her having on a different dress and shoes and that she had groomed herself. He recalled the other women in the community only changed their attire when leaving the house. Yet, she said she wasn't going out. He also remembered that the women in the other homes in the community where he had worked, never stayed in the home if they were alone. Well, she is different from them.

He stopped at McGillicudy's on the way home for a few slices of pizza and a beer. The popular saloon was busy at the earlier hour so he didn't get to discuss the events of the day with his longtime, bartender friend, as was their custom.

The following morning Rachel opened the door clutching a pink robe with furry white trim and matching slippers. Her hair was mussed and she looked sleepy.

"Oh, I'm sorry, Mrs. Sarnoff, ah, Rachel," said

Boyd, "I'm an early-bird, but I'll come at any time it's convenient for you and Mr. Sarnoff."

"No, it's all right. Without the children, and my husband not here, I overslept."

He walked over to the room where the work was to be done. He tacked a plastic sheet over the doorway to prevent dust from going into the rest of the house and began removing existing moldings.

About an hour later the plastic sheet was pushed aside. Rachel stepped in. She was dressed similar to the day before. Again not wearing the uniform-like housedress. Her wavy auburn hair had been curled and brushed, neatly framing her oval face, which showed a trace of makeup. She's really an attractive woman, he thought, and probably more so if she smiled.

"Would you like some coffee, Mr. Boyd?" she offered.

"No, but thank you. I always have a thermos of coffee in my van…Rachel" Thinking about her asking him to call her Rachel, he said, "Ah…why don't you call me Michael?"

"Very well, Michael." Boyd thought it was probably his imagination, but when he said he brings his own coffee, a look of displeasure crossed her face. She turned and let the plastic sheet fall back in place as she walked away. A minute later it was pushed back open. Rachel stood in the opening with the garage door remote in her hand. "You can use this garage door opener to let yourself in and out, we have extra."

"Thanks Rachel."

"I make fresh coffee every morning, so you don't need to bring your coffee."

"Sure…that'll be great, thanks."

I guessed that she was just trying to be accommodating and, like most clients, felt keeping their contractor happy pays out in better work.

Mid-morning of the following day, the plastic sheet parted. Rachel stood in the opening holding a mug of coffee. She was dressed nicely and again, not in the standard housedress. When he took the mug from her, he noticed her hand shook a little.

"Thanks."

She looked around for a moment, then turned and left.

A minute later the plastic sheet re-opened.

"I noticed Michael, that you don't stop for lunch."

"Sometimes I like to keep working."

"I thought you might like a sandwich for lunch."

"Well...sure. I would like to have a sandwich."

"I'll call when it's time."

He figured, with the home always empty she's lonely and could use some company and the reason for her offerings. He liked the idea of spending a little casual time with her and maybe satisfy his curiosity about her.

She called out that lunch was ready. He went into the bathroom and washed up. She was sitting at the table in the breakfast nook, opposite the place she had set for him, with a sandwich, a large pickle and a glass.

"This is very nice of you."

"Everything is Kosher. You couldn't tell the difference if I didn't tell you. I believe you construction men drink beer for lunch. I'm sorry but I don't keep any beer in the house. I do have iced tea."

"That'll be fine, thanks."

The lunch began on an awkward note with both of them eating quietly, not speaking.

Boyd broke the silence. "Great sandwich and terrific Kosher dills." She didn't say anything. To keep the conversation going, he said. "The cabinets will be delivered tomorrow. So it won't be too long before I'm finished."

"Fine, I'm looking forward to not working in the basement."

"Oh, no wonder I don't hear you anywhere in the house." He quickly regretted saying it. It sounded as though he was keeping tabs on her.

"Publishers send me articles, novels, advertising copy and I translate them into Yiddish." She paused. "Not so much for the little money it pays, it helps to pass the time I enjoy doing it." She paused. "It gives me an excuse not to socialize with the other women. They gossip, criticize their husbands, talk about where the best bargains are and play Mah Jong. It's not for me." She paused again. "Besides, they don't like me."

She saw the questioning look on Boyd's face.

"I'm younger than most of them and married to an older man. You can imagine how they talk. And I don't always follow the traditions. The women here do not stay alone in a house when a strange man is there. And have coffee and lunch together? Never! I'm what some people call a free spirit. To them, I'm a heretic. David approves everything I do. They think I've led him astray. At temple they ignore me. You can just imagine what they are saying about me now. But I don't care."

Boyd couldn't place her accent. He didn't think it would be proper to ask. Considering the informality created by their having lunch together, he decided it was okay to ask. "I notice you have a trace of an accent, Rachel."

"I'm Israeli…from Tel-Aviv. Twenty years now," Rachel freely offered. "My father and mother both taught English at Yeshiva. I met my husband, David, when he was vacationing in Israel. He was older but very charming. We married." She paused. "I had always wanted to go to America." She paused again. "The other women were all born here," she said, as if expanding on their detachment from her.

They were quiet for a few moments.

"So, now you know *my* story, Michael Boyd! What is yours?"

"Mine? Oh…nothing very interesting."

"Nothing interesting? I would think a man who has never married would be interesting."

"How did you know I was never married?"

"It's very obvious."

Obvious? He was puzzled by her comment but

didn't take it any further. "I need to get everything ready for the installation of the cabinets. I don't want your husband to be disappointed."

"My husband be disappointed?"

"Well, what I mean is, you and your husband— "

"Not to worry, he's very hard to disappoint. You have time. He won't be back for a few more days. He travels, giving seminars on taxes. He's very knowledgeable. He writes books."

"Still, I need to finish. I have another client on hold." He got up.

"Thank you for lunch."

"My pleasure," Rachel said without getting up. She made a small smile. Boyd thought it was the first time her expression had changed appreciably.

As he walked away, Boyd felt his pockets looking for his glasses. He'd only gotten them recently and was still not used to them. Only need them when I'm doing fine work or reading small print. I remember! I left them in my van again.

On the drive home, he was thinking about her. She's a married woman who sounds devoted to her husband. Yet, I feel as though I'll regret when I'm finished with the work and won't be seeing her anymore. Funny, how some people get into you psyche.

He didn't feel like cooking that evening and decided to stop at McGillicudy's, his favorite, and only haunt. He had about half his dinners there and almost all his Sunday dinners.

McGillicudy's was a unique restaurant. It had an Irish name but an Italian menu. It was located on a back road, yet it did an impressive business. Most of its customers were locals. The place was owned and operated by a father and son who inherited the business from the elder McGillicudy who had passed away. All three generations of the McGillicudy men, shared the same given name: William. 'Pops', the father, with a dour personality, ran the business. His son 'Juny' ran the busy bar.

Juny was a large, imposing, man, Boyd's age. Gregarious, a great storyteller, he gave the place its inviting atmosphere. The pizza and the authentic Italian fare was popular with the locals. Judging by how long the restaurant had been in business and the owners' comfortable lifestyles, it obviously did well. Whenever asked the frequent question about why a restaurant with an Irish name served only Italian food, Juny would happily explain, "Next to 'Eye-talians,' there's no one who appreciates pasta more than the Irish!"

Juny was married to Maria, a local girl of Italian ancestry. Pops was married to a native Italian, Concetta. They boasted publicly that the women made up the menu and did all the cooking. Privately, the cook Wong Hu, did all the food preparation from Concetta's ancestral recipes and she only oversaw the kitchen.

Maria, dark haired and olive-skinned, was in the restaurant just enough to give credibility to the Italian menu for which she unabashedly took all the credit. Their two sons, Mario and Sean, seven and nine year olds, were mischievous handfuls. Juny said they were that way because of their mixed Irish and Italian blood. They left Maria little time to participate in the operation of the restaurant.

Boyd and Juny graduated high school together and maintained a close personal friendship. Boyd's parents had passed away and his Sunday dinners were almost always at McGillicudy's, often, sitting at the family table. Weekday evenings when he dined at McGillicudy's, he dined at the bar. Juny would fend off inquiries from the single ladies asking about Boyd. He'd whisper to them that Boyd was just getting over a long-term relationship and wasn't ready yet. It was half true. Boyd's last relationship had ended two tears earlier. Juny's reason for keeping the interested women at bay was he felt he was saving them from disappointment. He knew Boyd all too well. Juny was Boyd's confessor, advisor and mentor. And being married, he considered himself an authority in matters concerning ladies and marriages.

"Michael m'boy! Haven't seen ya for a couple of days," he bellowed as Boyd sat. You're either working too hard or you've met someone," he said with a belly-shaking cynical laugh that indicated the latter was unlikely.

"Working, yes, the other? You know better!"

"Tell me what you're having," said Juny as he poured a draft and set it in front of Boyd. "And then you can tell me what it is that's bothering you."

"Bothering me? What makes you think that?"

"Michael, we've known each other since kindergarten. Need I say more? Besides, bartenders instinctively pick-up on stuff like that."

"There is something I'd like to talk to you about."

"I'm listening. First, let me take care of a customer."

Juny came back and leaned his elbows on the bar. "Let's hear it."

"There's this woman I'm doing some work for, Rachel…er, Mrs. Sarnoff—"

Juny raised the palms of his hands. "Hold on!"

"For what? I haven't told you anything yet!"

Juny squinted. "Is it Rachel…or Mrs. Sarnoff?"

"What's the difference?" Boyd shot back. "They're one and the same person!"

"B-i-i-i- i-g difference! So pick one or the other."

"Okay…Mrs. Sarnoff," said Boyd. He paused. "I don't know what there is about her, but she makes me feel confused."

"You're used to women coming on to you. You should know how to handle it."

"*Nooo*, it's nothing like that! She's married. Her husband's away on business and her kids recently left college. I guess she needs someone to talk to. She makes me coffee in the morning and today she made lunch. She told me about her life. She came here from Israel—"

Juny, again, raised his hand. "Tell me no more until next week."

"First you wanted to know, now you want to wait a week? Wait a minute…I think I know what you're getting at. You think I'm having a fantasy about her and I'll get over it in a week."

"Something like that. The bar's gotten busy. We'll have to continue this conversation next time," said Juny as he walked away, "I'm sure you'll have more to tell then."

When Boyd was home he listened to several messages on his answering machine. The last one said, "Michael. This is Rachel Sarnoff. Please give me a call."

He was alarmed. Why would she be calling me? Is there a problem with the work? He quickly called her back.

"Michael, you forgot your glasses. I thought you might not know where you left them and need them."

He breathed a sigh of relief. "I won't need them until I'm there tomorrow morning."

"No, I'm sorry. Tomorrow is the Sabbath. You can't work here."

"Oh, that's right, I forgot. I'll stop by early Sunday. I'll need them to read the Sunday paper."

"Sunday is fine," Rachel answered. She was silent for a moment. "I'll bring them over to you."

"No needs for you go out of your way. I can come get them."

"It will give me something to do."

"Well, if you wish to. I'll be here at one thirty. It's 427 Fischer Road, a rural road, off Mill Road about a mile from town. I'll wait for you by the mailbox in front of an old Victorian farmhouse."

After he hung up he thought about something. I remember leaving the glasses on top of my toolbox when I went out to the van to get some tools. Could she have—? But then, why would she? Juny's right, I'm really letting my imagination get carried away.

Driving back from Mass, he thought, it's only a little after one o'clock; I'll have time to change out of my Sunday church clothes. Don't want to give her the impression I got all dressed up for her.

Rachel was already there. Her black Mercedes was parked by the mailbox. She was standing outside the car, bundled up in a fur coat wearing high-heeled shoes. Her hands were in the pocket of the coat. Loose strands of her wavy auburn hair blew across her face. She waved a brown-gloved hand as his car approached.

He stopped his car in front of hers. He saw she had on lipstick, some eye makeup and rouge, looking attractive and much different than the woman he'd seen in the house.

"Oh, I'm sorry Rachel, I thought I said I'd be back at one thirty?"

"You did, Michael, but it's such a beautiful autumn day, I just wanted to get outside. So I bundled up and here I am." She paused. "I must say, you look quite nice. Very different in a sport jacket and a tie."

"My mother's idea."

A quizzical look came across Rachel's face.

"Oh, you live with your mother?"

"She passed away a few years ago."

Rachel was silent for a few seconds. "Oh yes, I understand."

She looked at his car.

"Such a sporty car. It goes well with your Sunday look."

"An old Mustang, had it for years. And I must say, you look quite nice yourself."

"Thank you," she smiled. Once in a while I like to look like something other than a kosher housewife."

She looked at the well-maintained old Victorian house that sat alone on the sparsely populated road. "So, this is where you live, Michael? It's a large house for a single person."

"Oh no. I don't live in the old farmhouse. The Fischer family lives here. At least they did until a few years ago when old man Fischer died. I just look after it for them. They come up from the city occasionally. Mostly in the summer."

Rachel's brow knitted. "Then why did we meet *here*, Michael?"

"I live here."

"Michael, you're getting me confused. I thought you said—"

"I live there," said Boyd as he nodded and pointed behind the old Victorian to a sturdy looking red barn in the middle of a mown meadow, well distanced behind the house.

"You live in a barn?"

"Yep."

"But barns have dirt floors and animals, and smell—"

"That's all true. Get in your car and drive behind me through the meadow up to the barn."

Boyd grinned seeing Rachel's puzzled look as she climbed into her car.

As they pulled up to the front of the barn the two big, wooden barn doors swung upward as a single unit. Inside was the white van, a tractor and a large travel-trailer.

Boyd got out of his car and walked over to Rachel's car. She stumbled towards him, her high heels sinking in the earth. He held out his arm to help her; she held on to it with her gloved hand.

As she entered the barn she looked around. "Oh, the floor is cement. I thought you said it was dirt."

He chuckled. "It *was* dirt. I poured a concrete slab over it."

"And you told me there were animals in here."

"Well, my car's a Mustang, the van's a work horse and the travel-trailer's a road hog," he said with a broad grin and a chuckle at his often used joke. And it stills smells like a barn! It's imbedded in the old wood."

"You certainly have a way of fashioning the truth, I must say," said Rachel, giving Boyd an ambivalent look. "So, Michael, you live in that trailer?"

"Occasionally."

"Occasionally?"

"You're getting ahead of me. Follow me."

He walked over to a door in the back wall, opened it and stepped aside to let her in. He flipped a light switch illuminating several large fluorescent-light fixtures hanging on chains from overhead ceiling beams. A completely outfitted woodworking shop filled with all different types of carpentry equipment. Bins held all manners of wood and other construction materials. Well-organized shelves held tools.

"Impressive; and so clean and orderly Michael," Rachel exclaimed. As her eyes perused the shop. She pointed to a cot set against one of the walls. "With your abilities and hard work, don't you deserve a better place to sleep?"

"I keep the cot in here because when I have a rush job and have to work through most of the night, I'll take cat-naps in it."

Rachel looked at him with knitted brow. "Michael, I'm still so confused. Where do you actually live?"

He held up a beckoning finger, walked over to a door on the side of the shop, opened it, reached inside and flipped up a row of switches.

"Let me take your coat," he offered as Rachel came through the doorway.

"Thank you, but it's chilly in here." She clutched the coat around her and stepped inside. She gasped and put a gloved hand over her mouth. Her eyes opened wide as she looked around. "Oh my!"

The room had a high, pitched ceiling — the underside of the barn's roof with exposed rafters of the original barn structure. The walls consisted of planed-down, knotty pine boards. There were mounted heads of deer, bear, fish and photographs of hunters and fishermen. The floor was made of wide boards.

"It looks like the inside of a barn, but then it doesn't," she said.

There was a billiard table and a poker table covered with green cloth surrounded by wood chairs and high stools. Tiffany-style lamps hang from long cords over the billiard and poker tables. Large round suspended globe lights also provided illumination. A sofa and several stuffed, brown leather chairs were placed randomly about the room next to which, were small, varnished, wood tables. The smell of wood permeated the space.

"This is all done by you?"

"Yep. And I have the calluses to prove it." He paused. "I sanded and varnished all the boards on the walls. The floor is made of oak plank, sanded and oiled." He grinned and said, "The furnishings are all store bought."

The wall at the rear had high windows, allowing the low winter sun to stream in, in shafts of sunlight warmed the room. A large, fieldstone fireplace climbed up between rafters and on through the roof. Split logs were stacked high alongside it.

"Lacking insulation, all windows face south to help the fireplace when needed."

"My goodness, Michael...this place is so beautiful!"

"You haven't seen it all, yet, Rachel."

Boyd took her hand. With her high heels tapping on the wood-plank floor, he led her through a large opening in the far corner of the rear wall. "This is the combination kitchen and dining room."

A lower ceiling there sloped to the rear of the space. The walls were of the same, wood plank, the floor was of large, flat bluestones. There were kitchen cabinets, cupboards of knotty pine and a chipped-tile countertop. And all the appropriate kitchen appliances.

In the middle of the kitchen was a long wood dining table with wood chairs, under a chandelier made from a wagon wheel. The far wall had several large windows allowing in the sun's rays making for a bright kitchen and dining space. A door in its middle led to an outside patio made of the same flat bluestone with a river stone barbeque in its middle." Al fresco dining," said Boyd.

"Michael, you did all this?"

"Who else," asked Boyd with a broad grin? "Except for the stone floors, plumbing and electric and tile work which was all bartered."

"Everything's been done with so much imagination."

A wood-paneled wall on the opposite side ran from the kitchen counter ran the entire length of the room. There were two side-by-side doors in the middle of it.

Rachel looked at the two doors in the middle of the opposite side, wall. "Let me guess, those lead to the only things I haven't yet seen; the bedroom and the bath."

"Good guess. The left door is to the bedroom with a bath and a large walk-in closet. The door on the right is my office."

He opened the door on the right and turned on a switch, lighting a large single, overhead, fluorescent-light fixture hanging in the middle of the room from a similar, sloped, lower ceiling.

Against the far wall were a drafting table with an attached, fluorescent fixture and a stool in front of it, facing a large window. Against one of the sidewalls were a reclaimed desk and a swivel chair. On the desk were a lamp, and numerous papers in a wire basket file along with customary desk items. Two old, also reclaimed looking wood filing cabinets flanked the desk.

The walls held a number of architectural drawings that were pinned open between n bookshelves that bulged with architectural and construction books and manuals. An Oak barrel held rolled up blueprints.

"Very impressive Michael. It looks more like an architect's office than that of home improvement person."

"In a way…it *is* an architect's office. After the Navy I went to college for 2 years under the G.I. bill and studied architecture, but I didn't have the funds to continue. However, I've put what I learned to good use for the jobs I work on.

"And those drawings of buildings on the wall?"

"Structures I hope to build some day."

Rachel stared at him. "There's more to you than meets the eye, Mr. Boyd."

"Why…thank you. Rachel."

"What meets the eye is also, quite impressive." Rachel said with a coy look.

Boyd's face flushed.

"You're blushing, Michael; how delightful!"

So, now, you're going to show me the bedroom and bath?"

"Ah-h…no! I'm not finished in there. It's still a work-in-progress."

"You're not hiding some young lady in there, are you, Michael? She paused and looked at him with an eyebrow raised. "I'm just teasing! My, how easy it is to make you blush."

"I'll outgrow it…someday."

"I'm sure all your efforts here will be rewarded when you sell the place."

"I don't own it."

Rachel looked surprised. "You don't' own it? Why then did you do so much work to it?"

"A number of reasons. Whenever I'm between jobs, it gives me something to do. Mr. Fischer pays for the materials. He trusts my judgment and gives me full design authority. His only restriction, it has to still look like a barn from the road. That's why the windows and everything are all in the back, on the south side. And I enjoy the challenge. Fischer said I could stay as long as I wanted without paying rent, just look after the old Victorian house and keep it in good shape. I feel it's a good trade-off."

"It seems with all the work you do, you hardly have time for anything else…or even to socialize." She hesitated. "I didn't mean to pry."

"I don't mind. In my free time I go fishing and hunting. I camp out on a large tract of land I own in the Adirondack Mountains. I hope to build my home up there, someday."

"Live up in the mountains?"

"Yep. That's where I want to be."

Boyd began closing things up. They walked back to the garage.

"It's all been very interesting, Michael."

Rachel waited for him outside the barn. Boyd came out and stood until the barn doors swung down and closed.

"I'll walk you to your car."

"But it's only right here, Michael."

"I mean I'll steady you on the high heels."

"Very thoughtful of you."

"And you are a very different woman from the one I know from the job."

"I like myself to be in both lives."

After Rachel started her car, she rolled down the window. They looked at each other in silence for a few moments.

"Thank you for the tour. Enjoy the rest of the day."

"Yes…you too…Rachel."

Rachel rolled up the window and started to back away, Boyd called out on an impulse, "You said you didn't have anything to do why don't you join me for Sunday dinner? I owe you a meal, you know," he said as if in explanation of his offer.

She stopped the car and rolled down the window back down. "I'd really like to, Michael, but

I wouldn't want to take a chance to be seen by my neighbors. It would make for more gossip."

"Where we'll go is off the beaten path. And very un-kosher. Highly unlikely there'd be anyone there who'd know you."

Rachel was quiet for a moment. "Oh, why not! I'll go! And you don't owe me a dinner. But you do owe me something else."

"I do? What is that?"

"Your life story, remember?" she said with a smile.

"Oh, yes, that! Follow me. The place we're going to is called McGillicudy's. It's my favorite eating place."

"I've never heard of it."

"I'm sure you haven't," said Boyd with a smirk.

As he drove with Rachel following behind him, thoughts swirled around in his mind. She looks, acts, so different than the person in the house. Much warmer and happier, too. She's charming and very attractive!

Parked at the restaurant he got out of his car and opened the car door for her. She stood up. They stood close, facing each other, smiling.

"I never knew this place was here. It's as you said, secluded."

"And not so busy on Sunday afternoons."

She held out a gloved hand, he took it in his and they walked to the entrance. As they stood inside the door, Juny, who is sitting at the family table, saw them and walked quickly over to them past the few occupied tables.

"Do you have a reservation, sir? I'm William and I'll be your waiter this afternoon." Rachel looked puzzled. Boyd and Juny began laughing. Rachel caught on.

"I'm called Juny. I don't believe we've met, Miss—?"

"Rachel," Boyd filled in.

"I'd invite you to sit with us at the family table but we're entertaining some friends." He whispered, "And four, very active kids. You can sit anywhere you wish."

Rachel looked toward a table in the far corner.

As Juny held the chair for her he looked over at Boyd, smiled broadly and shook his head up and down in admiration of the attractive woman and quickly turned to a frown and slowly moved his head from side-to-side as if to say, 'I hope you know what you're doing, Boyd.' "You know our Sunday Special Boyd, so I'll leave you be." He turned and walked away.

Boyd helped Rachel take off her coat. She removed her gloves and put them in one of the coat's pockets. He placed the coat over an empty chair. Rachel was wearing a dark blue, form fitting, velvet dress with a high neckline, long sleeves. It revealed a slim, curvaceous body. She wasn't wearing any rings or other jewelry.

"You look very nice, Rachel."

"Thank you, Michael. I only wear this dress for Bar Mitzvahs and Bat Mitzvahs, weddings… and special occasions." She paused. "I just felt in the mood to wear it today," she said with a slightly embarrassed look.

Juny had seated them sitting side-by-side as he customary did with dating couples. Boyd began to feel slightly uncomfortable. Being out with a married woman was something he'd never done before but assured himself it was all very innocent.

Juny came back holding a bottle of unopened red wine. "This is the house's finest Chianti." He held it out for them to read the label.

"Do you carry Manischewitz wine?" Boyd asked.

"I'm afraid we don't."

"The Tuscany wine will be fine," said Rachel.

"You're familiar with the origin of the wine?"

"Michael, I wasn't raised in a kibbutz. My parents were in academia. Summers, we traveled all over Europe. When David and I traveled, we were inclined to modify our religious beliefs and enjoy ourselves." She paused. "I'm sure you Catholics do the same. Otherwise, you wouldn't have need for confession." She smiled, seeming to enjoy her irreverent comment.

Juny returned with the wine bottle wrapped in a cloth and two glasses. He uncorked it and handed Rachel the cork and she examined it.

"Michael doesn't know from wines," said Juny as he poured a little wine in her glass.

Rachel held the wine glass by the stem, swirled it around, sniffed it and took a sip.

"You may pour the wine, sommelier," Rachel said in faked snobbishness.

"Thank you Mah-dum," responded Juny as he

poured the wine. "Enjoy," he said.

"I shall return shortly with the Sunday Special dinner."

They touched glasses and took sips, looking at each other over the tops of their glasses.

Boyd found the difference between the woman of the house and the worldly, charming woman sitting opposite him to be very intriguing. As though it was two different women.

"On Sundays, they always serve a single entrée," Boyd explained, "Lasagna. Between antipasto to insalata."

"And now Michael Boyd, it's time for your story. Or at least begin it while we wait for our dinner."

Boyd spoke about where he was raised, his father's early demise, his mother's working to feed them, his years in the Navy, his college years and establishing his business.

He ended with, "That's it in a nutshell. Not real interesting. Very ordinary, actually."

"Well, everything is relative. But there is something missing in your life story.

"Like what?"

"There has to have been some romance in your 38 years?"

Boyd was taken aback by her frank, inquisitiveness. It gave him pause.

"Well, Michael?"

He was trying to decide if he should open up to her about that part of his life. He felt he had adequately summarized his life; the parts which were responsible for who he was. They had become comfortable and trusting with each other and he didn't want her to think he was some sort of a celibate.

"Well…I dated a lot, but there was this…one girl."

Rachel set her glass down on the table, seeming anxious to hear what he had to say.

"Noreen Fitzgerald. She came from Southern Ireland, a friend of the McGillicudy's relatives in Ireland. She was 27 years old, raised on a sheep farm, college educated and a schoolteacher in Ireland. She wanted more than being an 'Irish school marm'…as she put it. So she came to America five years ago to teach here.

"She stayed at the McGillicudy family home and worked here as a waitress while trying to find employment in education. But she found to meet the local certification requirements she would have had to take some additional expensive, college courses. And that it would help if she got rid of her strong Irish accent

"Juny taught her to bartend. He boasted business increased 50% when she worked."

"What did she look like," Asked Rachel.

"Everyone said she strongly resembled the actress, Maureen O'Hara. Do you know her?"

"Vaguely."

"She was very pretty, that's for sure. Beautiful, actually; a lightly freckled face, strawberry-blond hair that curled off in every direction. Very Irish." Boyd became embarrassed by his overly inclusive description.

"So why did you not marry her?"

"We lived together for two years. In the barn while I was in the process of rebuilding it. She loved going up to the Adirondack property and camping in the trailer. She was a country girl at heart. We were great together. But as time went on she grew more and more disappointed because she wasn't achieving her American dream. Which involved teaching. She blamed it partly on her very pronounced Irish brogue. I helped her with her diction, but she made slow, painful, progress. We were both busy and couldn't devote much time to it. Sometimes she'd get so frustrated about it she would spout out in a Gaelic tirade."

"I think I can relate to that," said Rachel nodding. She paused. "I can tell by the expression on your face as you spoke of her, she meant a lot to you. What happened to her?"

"I came home to the barn one day and I saw that her belongings were gone. I rushed over here to look for her. Juny came over and put his hand on my shoulder and said, 'She's gone, gone back home to Ireland. I'm sorry, Michael.'"

"He gave me her address in Ireland. She only answered my first letter, saying the only way we could be together was I would have to come and live in Ireland. I told her I couldn't do that and that she should come back and give it another try. I never heard from her again. Despite all my letters and unanswered phone calls."

"How sad, Michael," Rachel reached out and

puts her hand on his arm. "At some point in our lives, we all meet up with some form of disappointment in love."

Boyd had the feeling that Rachel wanted to reveal a disappointment of her own. He opened up an opportunity for her. "I don't suppose you've ever had to go through something like that, Rachel?"

Rachel's face became somber. She stared off in space. "I am about to face a similar crisis."

"Would you like to talk about it?" Boyd offered. "You don't have to. I know how hard it is to talk about something like that. Just as it was for me."

"Yes, I would like to speak about it, Michael. It's one of the reason's I'm glad we're here."

"Go ahead, I'm a good listener."

She was silent and contemplative for a few long moments. "David and I are to be divorced." Her tone was surprisingly indifferent for such a matter of seriousness."

"Well that certainly is a crisis! Breaking up with a girlfriend is one thing, divorcing, that's a whole other thing."

"Michael, it's not the divorce that's the crisis."

"I don't understand."

"David and I agreed to divorce, years ago, but not until the children were off to college. It was… and is…going to be amicable. He's a wonderful man and he said he would be fair with me. I know he means it."

She paused, looking thoughtful. "He has a wonderful woman, his office manager. They've been a business team for many years. She's very understanding, and patient, and a very nice person. They're also closer in age. They belong together."

"Where's the crisis, then? It seems you've both worked everything out."

"The crisis? The crisis is me."

"I think I understand. You're still in love with David."

"As a person, yes, but I don't love him as a wife, as a woman should."

"I'm still confused, Rachel."

"Michael, I'm 37 years old. Unqualified for most any work other than the translating I have been doing. It's sporadic and doesn't pay very well. Not nearly enough to support me."

"But your husband…David…said he'd be fair to you. From what little I know about him, he's a man of some wealth. The law entitles you to a good portion of it; possibly let you keep the house."

"I don't want the house. He and his future wife do." She paused, looking troubled. "What I need is self-esteem. Not money, not a house. Self esteem! And I have no idea where, how get it, how to find it."

"No offense Rachel, but I think you need to see a therapist."

"I already did."

"And how did that go?"

"She practically threw me out of her office, implying there are people who really need her help and I was not one of them!" Rachel paused. "She had gone through a divorce and wasn't very empathetic."

"But now let's do what we came here for. Mangia! As the McGillicudy women say. Wait until you try the McGillicudy food starting with the antipasto special' followed by the lasagna. You did say said you do skip Kosher on special occasions."

"Yes. And this is definitely a special occasion. I can't wait to have…what you said."

"From here on Rachel, it's all happy talk."

"You first!" Rachel quickly answered.

They both broke out laughing.

"There's nothing I like better than being with a beautiful, intelligent woman with a sense of humor."

Her face beamed at the compliment. "Michael, I really appreciate your inviting me to see your wonderful barn and dining here with you. It really is something I needed."

"Glad to accommodate. Especially when there are so many benefits in it for me as well."

The afternoon in McGillicudy's ended with the two of them standing alongside Rachel's car in the parking lot. She reached for Boyd's hand and held it. "I had a wonderful afternoon, Michael. Thank you so much for showing me the barn. And the wonderful dinner and everything else. I hope we can do it again, sometime."

"Oh sure, we definitely should. And will."

"I'll see you – I look forward to seeing you at my house in the morning." Rachel got into her car, Boyd gave her directions and she backed out. As she pulled away, she gave Boyd a wave and smile.

Boyd stared at the car as it drove away. He

walked to his car. *I hope I know what I'm doing. She's a troubled woman who is still living with her husband! I have to think this all through before we take it any further. Because that's where it looks like it's going.*

The following morning as he dressed, he couldn't help thinking what it was going to be like when he and Rachel were in the house together. In a single day their relationship had completely changed.

He used the remote to open the garage door of the house. David Sarnoff was standing just inside.

"Ah-h, good morning, Mr. Sarnoff," Boyd said uneasily.

"Good morning to you Mr. Boyd, how are you today?" he said, pleasantly.

"I'm fine, fine thanks."

Sarnoff followed him as he took his toolbox out of the truck.

"Everything looks very good. I understand you're ready for the cabinets, eh?"

"Pretty much. Just a few minor odds-and-ends to do today."

"Mr. Boyd, I waited here because there something I wish to speak to you about," said Sarnoff, sounding serious.

A chill ran up the uncomfortable Boyd's back. "Sure, Mr. Sarnoff."

"Call me David, please. And if I may, I'd like to call you Michael."

"Sure."

"When we bought this house the builder only finished half the basement. I would like you to complete it just like the finished half."

A feeling of relief came over Boyd.

"I don't know when I would be able to start; I have some other jobs waiting."

"Not a problem. There's no rush, Michael. I'll go back to my breakfast."

Boyd wondered if Rachel had told him they had spent the previous day together.

There wasn't any way to tell from their discussion. From what Rachel had told him about their marriage status he saw no reason for her not to. Nonetheless, he was uncomfortable.

Shortly after he started working, he heard the garage door open. He looked out the window and saw Sarnoff backing out his car. The plastic sheet opened; Rachel was standing just inside in the pink bathrobe. Her face looked freshly scrubbed and she didn't have any makeup on. She looked different but as pretty as the day before when she was all dressed up.

"Good morning, Michael," she said warmly.

Without returning the greeting, "Did you tell… tell him about our spending the day together?"

Rachel frowned. "There's no reason I should or shouldn't tell him. I told you of our situation. I haven't seen him today. He came home after I was asleep. We sleep in different rooms. He fixed his own breakfast. Normally, I do." She paused. "You seem out of sorts, Michael, are you all right?"

"I'm fine, really."

The smile returned to her face. "I really enjoyed being with you yesterday, Michael. I haven't felt so good in a long time."

"Yeah, me too."

"I'm in such a good mood today. I'm going to fix us a special lunch." The plastic sheet closed and she was gone.

Boyd wasn't sharing her joyful mood. He had no idea where this was all going. Or if he even wanted to get involved with her. We're people from two different worlds.

His mind turned to Noreen. They too came from different worlds and that went well until—. But they shared a lot of common interests; camping, fishing, skiing. The only reason it ended was because she couldn't fulfill her dream of becoming a teacher. It wasn't about him.

He heard Rachel going into the basement. Shortly afterward he heard the phone ring. He could hear she was on the phone where she stayed most of the morning.

Just before noon he smelled eggs cooking. Rachel called out, "Lunch is ready!" He went into the bathroom and washed up. When he walked into the kitchen, he saw she had everything prepared on the breakfast counter. He sat.

She was still wearing her robe and slippers. "Sorry, I didn't have a chance to change. I got a call from my publisher. He had a rush assignment we were able to do over the phone. I hope you don't mind," she said as she pulled her robe closer around her. On the breakfast nook table was a vegetable and cheese omelet with hash brown potatoes, orange juice and coffee.

"Sit, enjoy." She sat and put a napkin in her lap. "Hope you like it. I'm sure you'll miss the bacon, but the smell would get out into the neighborhood."

They ate quietly having already touched on so much the previous day. Their common interests were limited.

Rachel kept looking across the table at him. He smiled back to assure her he was enjoying the food. "It's really excellent, Rachel. Even without bacon."

"I'm glad you're enjoying it. I am a good cook even though I have to prepare food within the dietary restrictions." She paused. "Michael, do you suppose Juny would share their lasagna recipe with me?"

"He would., but then he'd have to kill you."

"Wha…what?" Rachel said looking shocked.

"An old joke," said Boyd with a chuckle. "Someone will say that when they don't wish to share a secret. But not being serious."

"Oh … you scared me." Rachel began describing how she might try to make kosher lasagna. In her exuberance she hadn't noticed her robe had fallen open at the bosom, revealing she wasn't wearing anything underneath.

Boyd pointed to his chest. She looked at him quizzically then caught on, looked at her chest and pulled the robe together. "Oh, I'm sorry. I hope you didn't think—"

Boyd shook his head.

Soon as they'd finished lunch, Boyd rose. "Hate to eat and run but I need to finish today's work. The cabinets are being delivered tomorrow morning. Thanks for the lunch. And you are a good cook."

"Michael, before you leave, there's something I'd like to ask you," Rachel said, looking intense.

"Yes?"

She was quiet for a few moments. "Would you…would you take me with you when you go up to your mountain property?"

It took Boyd by surprise. He didn't immediately know how to respond.

Rachel smiled. "I could cook for you."

Boyd just looked at her. He had no ready answer.

"Michael, I…I really need to get away for a few days."

"I have to think about it, Rachel."

"I understand, Michael." She was quiet for a moment "I could stay in a nearby motel. I just need to spend some time away from here. And there's no one else I could…rather be with."

"Let me think about it, Rachel."

Boyd walked over to the room he was working in.

He went about the work listlessly; his mind was preoccupied. He admitted he was drawn to her. It had been a long time since enjoyed the company of a woman. And one who appealed to him as much as Rachel. But I've only known her for days.

And cavorting with a married woman has never

been my thing. I know she said that she and Sarnoff have an understanding. But they could change their minds. But should *I* make an issue of it? It's really not my problem. Or is it?

He could hear her in the kitchen clearing the dishes and starting the dishwasher. He heard her go downstairs and begin speaking on the phone.

He wondered if not giving her an answer about going away together would end their relationship. The thought bothered him. He knew he'd like more of her company, but on terms they both could be comfortable with.

At the end of the day he packed up his tools and went downstairs to go out through the garage to his truck. As he was about to push the button to raise the garage door, it suddenly began to rise. On the outside was Sarnoff in his car. They waved to each other as he drove into the garage. Boyd thought it was early for him to be home.

As Boyd loaded his tools in the back of the van, he was startled by Sarnoff's voice coming from behind him. "Michael, could I have a moment with you, please?"

"Oh-h…sure…David."

He was hoping he just wanted to speak to him about the work. But he had a gut feeling it wasn't. Boyd looked at the man in the black overcoat and the black fedora. Despite his serious tone, Sarnoff had a pleasant look on his face.

"Michael, can we take a little walk together?"

"Sure…David," said Boyd, trying to sound casual. "Let me get my jacket. He walked around to the front of the truck, took his jacket out. As he was putting it on, Sarnoff walked up next to him. Despite Sarnoff's pleasant demeanor, Boyd had a queasy feeling in the pit of his stomach. He recalled someone once saying, "When you're on a date with a married woman, you're a threesome."

They began walking side-by-side down the driveway toward the street. Sarnoff put his arm through Boyd's. The friendly gesture did little to ease Boyd's discomfort.

Sarnoff turned to him. "Michael, this afternoon Rachel called and discussed something with me."

Boyd turned and looked worriedly into the eyes of the man beside him.

"She told me about the wonderful time you two had together yesterday. And the most impressive barn you designed and renovated."

Although he was taken aback, Sarnoff's friendly tone calmed him some.

"She enjoyed the day immensely, it made her very happy." He paused. "She hasn't been happy for a long time. With the children gone, it's gotten worse. She said she explained our situation to you. But she feels that you are hesitant to spend time together which has made her unhappy, very unhappy."

"Well, uh-h…David, I really don't know what to say," Boyd stammered nervously."

"Michael, I have no problem with the two of you spending time together. As a matter-of-fact, I completely approve of it and I too would be happy if you did. She well deserves it. She feels that you enjoy her company but have your…values. She too is a woman of values, of faith. However, that she likes to modify it occasionally. I believe you've already experienced it," he said with a chuckle in his voice.

Boyd, very much relieved, smiled. "Yes, I have."

"Now that the children are on their own, we are going to carry out our divorce." He hesitated. "To do so, one of us must return to Israel. Of course, it must be her. What I'm saying is, before she leaves, I hope you can establish your relationship, and that you can share time together." He paused. "I'm happy and I want her to be happy. She is a good woman."

Driving home, Boyd's mind was in turmoil. He was involved in something he never had happen before. I'm left with two choices. We go on the camping trip or totally end the relationship. With a woman like her, going away together establishes a… commitment.

He decided they would do the camping trip and felt good about the decision.

The following morning when he entered the garage, Sarnoff's car was gone. When he was upstairs, he didn't see Rachel or hear her. Later in the morning he heard her in the kitchen and smelled coffee. The plastic sheets parted, Rachel entered, dressed in the typical housedress. She was holding two mugs of coffee. As she handed one to him, he saw her hand was shaking.

"Coffee, the way you like it, Michael."

"Thanks, Rachel."

She sipped her coffee, staring over the cup at him. Sipping his, he stared back. For a few long moments an awkward silence existed.

"Rachel, how are you fixed for camping clothes?"

Her face blossomed in color, her eyes opened wide. She rushed toward him, dropping her cup, letting it smash on the floor and threw her arms around him with such force his coffee splashed on him.

"Oh, I'm very sorry, I just got so excited." She paused. "I'll be good…I promise. No, I don't have any camping outfits."

"There's a great country store for camping outfits up there."

"I'll bring the marshmallows," said the happy woman.

"It'll be on Thanksgiving weekend which is only a week and a half away."

Each day Boyd wouldn't see Rachel until mid-morning when she came into the room with mugs of coffee. She'd be dressed in the bland housedress, but her face would be glowing. Her hands no longer shook when she handed him the coffee. They drank their coffee sitting on newly arrived furniture crates. She was bright and cheerful, and complimenting of his work.

She made lunch each day. On a few evenings

she made dinner for them. They discussed their upcoming camping weekend in the Adirondacks.

"Michael, tell me about your place in the mountains."

"That would spoil the pleasure of when you first see it. It's only days away."

A few days later the remodeling work in the Sarnoff home was completed. Boyd spent the days before their trip working on the barn's bedroom and bath. Not seeing her as much as when working in the home made him want to be with her even more. On several occasions when David wasn't coming home for dinner, she had Boyd over.

One evening when he went to McGillicudy's for dinner, he told Juny of his long Thanksgiving weekend plans with Rachel.

"Whaddayathink Juny?"

Juny cocked an eyebrow and squinted at him with the other eye. A familiar look that meant an unfavorable opinion was forthcoming.

"Ya know Michael," Juny began. "I've always been very opinionated about the girls you spent time with. But this lady is an unknown quantity to me. I only know what you tell me about her and what I saw the one time she was here. On the surface, I don't like it. Granted, she's attractive, intelligent and personable. But let's not forget, she's different…very different!" He hesitated. "I'm sorry, but I just can't see you two together." He paused looking Boyd straight in the eyes. "That's all I'm gonna say about her."

"I appreciate your frankness, Juny, I really do. You're right, we're a whole world apart and she is different from the other girls I've known. That's for sure."

"Ya know, Boyd, your biological clock is ticking. Ya gonna hafta marry pretty soon if there's to be any little Boyd's."

"That biological clock thing is for women, Juny." Juny leaned over the bar and looked squinty-eyed, directly into Boyd's eyes. "The woman you'll marry will be about your same age, so, yes, her clock will be ticking too. I don't expect your gonna marry some young chippee." He leaned back. "Do ya think you would ever really give serious thought to marrying?"

"Sometime, I guess I will, Juny, sometime."

"Hah! That I gotta see," said Juny and walked away to serve a customer.

It was the morning of the Wednesday before Thanksgiving. The day they planned to leave for the Adirondack property.

Rachel's black Mercedes rolled up to the barn where Boyd was taking work items out the back of the van replacing them with the camping gear and other necessities. He was wearing a plaid shirt with a tan hunting vest over it, camouflage–print cargo trousers tucked into low boots, and a camouflage-styled, hunting cap.

"My, you look so outdoorsman," said a smiling Rachel as she got out of her car and walked up to him. She was wearing fleece-lined, leather windbreaker with a black, wool scarf, a long leather skirt over heavy black with a black, stockings and walking shoes. She had on some lipstick and eye makeup and looked attractive – which gained an admiring look from him.

"I like your outfit. I know you didn't pull it from one of your closets."

"I did some shopping. Do you like it?"

"Yes, I do. It should keep you warm for the trip, but you'll need headgear."

"I have a fur hat in the car with my small travel-bag…and marshmallows," she tittered happily. "I didn't want to wear the hat and muss up my hair. I want to look as nice as I can for you."

"You don't need to worry about that."

"Can I help with anything?"

"Not just yet. Right now, I need to load all the heavy stuff; generator, gas cans, and a long heavy-duty electric cable. Things we need to be comfortable. Though I love camping, I still like to have my creature comforts."

"Michael, please don't change things for me. I'm only coming for…as they say, for the ride."

The comment made them both stare coyly at each other.

"I'll be staying overnights at a motel, won't I?" She paused. "The trailer is really only one room."

"Plenty big enough for the two of us," he said as he continued with the loading. He looked back at her to see the effect his answer had on her. He saw a Quixotic look and a smile. He was glad to see she was happy and knowing that he was responsible.

"We need to hook the house trailer onto the van. I'll pull it out after I move the Mustang then we'll put your car inside."

"My, there's certainly a lot of work to do when one goes camping."

"It's routine. I'm used to it. When you enjoy what you're doing, work can be fun."

"A great attitude, Michael!" She paused. "I won't miss not having a Thanksgiving turkey."

"Not have Thanksgiving turkey? No way! I have one in the cooler. It's small enough to fit in the trailer's oven. And, I have all-l-l the trimmings!"

"You are an amazing man, Mr. Boyd."

She carried a box of groceries into the van. When she came out of it, she said, "My, it's very… ah, cozy."

"It will be," he said with a sly grin.

The trip to the Adirondacks would take four hours. Boyd had brought sandwiches a thermos filled with hot coffee; a box of donuts, and a selection of music tapes. Earlier on into the trip they both were quiet enjoying the passing countryside, listening to the music tapes. Occasionally, they'd turn and look at each other and smile; but with questioning looks in their eyes – as though they were both thinking the same thing.

Boyd patted the space on the seat between them. She slid over close to him.

"Can I ask you something Rachel? She glanced at him with a wary look.

"What is it, Michael?"

"I don't mean to pry, but from what you've told me, you and David have been living under the same roof but not as husband and wife?"

"Yes. In separate bedrooms. For many years now," said Rachel, somberly.

"That means you haven't had…relations?"

"Michael! Please! You're embarrassing me!" said Rachel as she pushed herself away from him.

"Heck! It's not much different than my own situation."

"Michael! Can we change the subject?"

Boyd grinned and muttered under his breath, "This should be one heckova weekend!"

Rachel heard him, and glanced at him with a demure, almost frightened, look. Boyd turned to her and smiled. Rachel returned the smile and moved back up close to him. She held his arm with both her hands and leaned her head against his shoulder.

As they got further into the trip and through the less urban areas, they were treated to spectacular views of trees bearing their waning autumn colors. They drove through picturesque country villages sitting along the foothills of the mountains. Their enjoyment of the scenic countryside made the trip go fast. About the time the coffee was finished, and the sandwiches and half the donuts eaten, Boyd turned off the paved road on to dirt, back road.

"We're on the home stretch", he announced as the van's wheels rumbled on the earthen road.

"It went so quickly," said Rachel looked at Boyd

and smiled. "Time flies when you're…happy."

They drove uphill for a while then turned into a barely identifiable roadway, went a short distance and pulled onto a large flat, mowed meadow at the edge of a plateau. Rachel stared wide-eyed through the windshield at the distant mountains.

"Michael, this, this place is absolutely magnificent!"

"Glad you like it. There's a few more hours before sunset. We'll take a walk around and take in the scenery. Then I'll set up the trailer on the concrete slab I installed, which one day will be part of the house."

Holding hands, they walked to the edge of the plateau, which sloped steeply down to a rushing stream. They took in the mountainous panorama.

"It's breathtaking, Michael, so beautiful. I can't blame you for wanting to live here someday."

"That's a great trout fishing stream down there. We'll give it a try soon."

"Your property, it' so perfect; and so pristine."

"I had it bulldozed level and planted some wild-grass seed. A local farmer mows it."

Boyd maneuvered the trailer onto the concrete slab and began to level it up.

"I'll wait until tomorrow before setting up the generator and unloading everything. There're other priorities that need attending."

"Speaking of priorities," Rachel asked, "I assume we have a bathroom?"

"Oh sure, there's two of them."

"Two bathrooms?"

"Yep! One's inside the camper, the other's outside."

"Outside?" Rachel looked puzzled. "Ohhh, I understand."

"With campers, the usual contained necessities, water and waste disposal are normally limited.

"You mean we have to be careful using—?"

Boyd shook his head. "I had an artesian well drilled and a septic system installed, both adequate to accommodate my future house. And for now, used for trailer living."

"My goodness, Michael, you've really thought ahead."

"I'll hook into them now." He walked over to a small steel cover on the corner of the slab, opened it to reveal two pipe connections. Rachel followed him "One's the water, the other leads to the septic system. I'll hook the trailer into them, and then we can go about our…business." He chuckled at his play on words.

Rachel went inside the trailer and looked around. "It's like a little house, Michael it has everything," she called out.

"I may like camping, but I like being comfortable as well."

"That is something I like to hear," said Rachel.

Boyd went over to a corner of the meadow and carried split wood to circle of fieldstones about 2 feet high with an iron grill on top, "The farmer leaves me wood to barbeque with. I'll get a fire going. Tonight's special is beef patties, cheddar cheese, red onions, inside sesame seed buns with sides of German potato salad. Washes down with ice cold Heinekens. But if you prefer, you can eat your marshmallows."

"Michael, you're such a tease."

"I have a couple lawn chairs in the storage compartment in the under-part of the trailer. We'll cook dinner on the barbeque and dine al fresco using my finest plastic dinnerware, watching the sun set behind the mountains."

"My, you are so organized!"

As darkness set in, and the meal was finished, the fire from the barbeque cast an eerie glow on the surrounding trees. Rachel moved her chair closer to Michael's and put her arm through his.

"The temperature's dropped. Are you cold?"

"The cold doesn't bother me. But are there bears in these woods?"

"Bears are pretty lethargic this time of year. Pretty fattened up, getting ready to hibernate."

"Would they try to kill us?"

"Only to get at the food. We could always defend ourselves by throwing the marshmallows at them."

"Michael, you're not taking it serious."

"Well, if it makes you feel better, I have my hunting rifle handy. Let's go inside. It's gets pretty cold at night in the mountains."

"Do you think you should drive me to that motel we passed by?"

"No! You're going to stay here."

"But I only saw one bed, a double bed."

"It's big enough for—"

"Michael, you must understand. I have, my faith, moral standards which I—"

"Yes, I do understand, but since I won't be able to hook up the generator tonight, it's going to get pretty cold in there. We'll need each other's body heat."

"Michael, are you listening to me?

"We'll have to sleep fully clothed. That should keep us warm … and on the straight-and-narrow."

"I suppose," said Rachel, sounding skeptical.

"Did it with one of my hunting buddies. Worked fine."

She looked askance at him. "That is an odd comparison!"

"Yes, it is…you'll smell a lot better."

"Michael!"

"Actually, the little sofa pulls out into a second bed. We'll use that for when we have heat. Does that make you feel better? "

"I will let you know in the morning," she answered with a coy expression.

When they were inside he took four short, fat, candles from a cabinet, placed them around the camper and lit them.

"My, how … romant … how nice," cooed Rachel.

"Well, they'll give off some heat."

"Heat? " she questioned looking skeptical.

"Ah…I meant for light for during the night. It's been a long day. We better hit the hay."

They got into bed under a heavy blanket, fully

clothed with only their boots and shoes off. Facing each other, they fell asleep.

The morning sun was streaming through the camper's windows.

"How'd you sleep?" Michael asked.

"Very well … considering. But I would like to shower."

"I'll get the generator going right away so we can have heat and hot water and have breakfast," said Michael. "I was planning on bacon and eggs. Are you kosher or non-kosher this trip?"

"If I was your prisoner, I wouldn't have a choice, would I? In a way, I am your prisoner."

"Hm! I kind of like that idea! As long as you don't report me to the authorities. Bacon it is. We'll keep breakfast light and save room for the turkey and the trimmings."

"I'll cook," offered Rachel.

"No, in the camper I do the cooking. It's a little different than cooking at home."

"You sure know the way to a lady's heart Michael…in more ways than one. But I'd like to make some contribution, Michael."

"Washing dishes is permissible."

"Gladly."

They sat in the small dining nook having breakfast.

"There's nothing like the fragrant smell of bacon to make a place feel homey," offered Boyd.

"Yes, but I'll have to get the smell out of my

clothes before I'm back home."

"Not to worry. I do the laundry in the local Laundromat while I'm shopping in town." He paused. "It's a beautiful clear day and not so cold. How do you feel about going on a hike while the turkey's cooking?"

"What about the bears?"

"As I said, this time of year they are preparing for their hibernation."

"Then they might want to eat us?"

"No, they're vegetarians. They will get aggress when they think you're after their food or when they're protecting cubs. I'll bring along my 457 Magnum pistol, just in case. It's still the hunting season so we'll need to wear fluorescent-red vests."

"It sounds scary, but I trust your judgment," she said as she gazed admiringly at him.

Boyd prepared the turkey for cooking and put it in the oven.

They walked arm-in-arm along the continuation of the dirt road taking in the scenery and the sounds.

Rachel looked up at Boyd. "Michael."

"Yes? "

"You're so self-reliant, a free spirit. Do you think…you'll ever marry?"

"Hm! The familiar getting married, question. Are you proposing?"

"Oh, I'm sorry, I didn't mean to pry." She hesitated. "But did someone ever ask you to marry?"

"Only Juny, but he's not my type." Boyd quipped. He put his finger teasingly on Rachel's nose. "To answer the question…sure. Almost everyone, female or male, does get asked sooner or later." He looked at Rachel to see her reaction to his vague answer.

A puzzled, bemused smile came across her face.

"Turkey's done," called out Boyd as he peered into the oven and pulled the bird out. "That little oven does a great job. Now that we're done cooking, I'm going to shut off the generator and get rid of the noise."

Rachel filled dishes with Boyd's 'fixen's' and they slid into the dining nook and dug in.

"Michael, this turkey is as good as any I have ever tasted."

As she ate, Rachel stared at Boyd.

"Why are looking at me like that?"

She didn't say anything, just shook her and smiled.

"The camper will remain warm enough through the day. I'll put it back on for while before we go to bed. We don't want the noise during night when we're trying to sleep. With help from the blanket and our body heat, we won't have to go to bed dressed like Eskimos again."

"Michael, I don't want to disappoint, but I'm afraid I can't do—"

"I understand." He hesitated. "And I'm not even sure I could, either."

Rachel stared at him as if pondering what he said. "I believe you are still mending over your… Noreen."

"Let's not bring her into—. This getaway is about us." He paused. "I'll sleep on the settee pull-out bed. I think we'll both feel better about it."

She looked at him with saddened eyes. "I'm not sure I can say I'll feel better about it."

The following morning after a bacon and eggs breakfast, they dressed appropriately and headed downhill to get to the stream.

"I've never done anything like this before," called out Rachel, breathlessly as they neared the sound of the rushing water. "It's so exhilarating. Even if we don't catch any fish, it's an experience just being here."

"Oh, we'll catch some all right. We eat what we catch. Fish grilled on the fire make for a great meal."

Boyd taught Rachel to cast. He snared four good-sized trout. With each catch, Rachel squealed with glee. "Imagine! Actually eating food you caught, yourself. It's so … natural."

"Yes, but hunting deer produces months worth of dinner meat."

"I can't imagine killing those beautiful animals."

"That's called the Bambi syndrome. But no one feels the same way for the fish. Guess it's 'cause you don't look the fish square in the eyes while they're alive. All meat comes from some animal. Even Kosher—"

"Enough said, Michael."

That evening they dined on the fish cooked

over the open fire along with the leftovers from the Thanksgiving meal.

When they arose in the morning, everything outside was covered with a light dusting of snow.

"Oh, Michael, it so picturesque."

"You know what to do when it's snow-covered? You make tracks in it. Suit up and let's hit the trail."

Rachel was putting things away as Boyd was hooking the camper up to the truck. "Got everything back in place and we are ready to go. Can't say I'm happy about it the weekend being over." He was quiet for a few moments. "I feel like I wish it wouldn't end."

"Michael, this is a Thanksgiving I will never forget. A weekend I'll always remember.

"Rachel, we'll do it again, I promise."

"I'd like to believe that."

They came together and kissed, a long loving kiss.

Rachel was sitting in her car outside the barn waiting for it to warm up. She rolled down the window as Boyd walked over. "Thanks for your help putting things away."

"Michael, I cannot even begin to tell you what wonderful time I had."

They stayed quiet for a few long moments, just staring into each other's eyes. Her face saddened. "Michael, I … I think I've fallen in—"

Boyd put his finger to her lips. "There's a time

for that … and it isn't now."

Rachel's eyes teared. She nodded and rolled the window and quickly backed her car out. Michael waved as he watched her drive away.

He turned and walked toward the barn, thinking, I've got to sort this all out. Sure, we had a great time and enjoyed each other's company. Still, we've only known each for only a short time. I can relate to where she's coming from…a lonely and needy place. That goes for me as well. In such a romantic setting, who wouldn't have felt they were falling in love? This relationship needs time. I'm willing to wait. But I'm not so sure she is.

He walked back to the barn with his down and shoulders in a slouch.

Not having any desire to cook for himself that evening, he decided to go over to McGillicudy's. Besides, he needed someone to talk to about the long weekend. And, who else but Juny?

He sat at his usual place at the bar.

"Well, Michael m'boy, tell me how your romantic weekend went?" asked Juny as he set a beer down in front of Boyd. "No, don't tell me, let me guess. It was divine, heavenly, marvelous, wonderful, and a whole lot of other words women like to use." He stopped. "Boyd! You should be smiling like the cat that ate the canary! What's the down look all about? Don't tell me it didn't go well!"

"No, it was great, better than great!" Boyd answered indifferently.

Juny cocked an eyebrow, squinted and smiled.

"It's not what you're thinking. We did have a great…you know…all those words you said. But things get complicated when two people are…you know."

"No I don't know—. Ya hafta tell me! Remember, I got married right after high school."

"It's a lot different when two adults come together," said Boyd solemnly, "adults with… histories."

Juny's expression went bland. "Ahh…speaking of history—" He hesitated for a moment. "I didn't want to tell you this right away. But Noreen's back!"

It took a few seconds for Juny's statement to penetrate through the confusion of thoughts that occupied Boyd's mind.

"She's…she's here?" said the stunned Boyd.

Well … not here. She had Thanksgiving dinner with us, then left and went back to New York City where she's living."

Boyd was silent. Juny didn't offer anything further.

"Living in the city? Since when? What's that all about? Did she ask about me?"

"Dumb question," Juny quickly retorted.

"What did she say? Why is she in the city? How long has she been back?"

"Those are questions you'll have to talk with her about. I don't want to repeat anything…maybe incorrectly and cause trouble."

"Trouble? Why should there be trouble? Is something wrong."

"No, no. In fact, everything is fine with her. She wants to see you. She has some … surprises. I'm sure she'd want to tell you yourself."

"Surprises? What kind of surprises?" He stopped. "She didn't get married or have a kid, did she?"

"Well, if she got married and had a kid, she didn't happen to mention it," Juny answered sarcastically. "Actually, all is good with her. Really! But you're gonna have to talk to her direct."

"How will I get to see her?"

"She said she'd be in Wednesday evening after work. Be here!"

"Working? Doing what?"

"Gimme your order," Juny growled.

"I'm not hungry."

"You're not gonna eat? We have pastafazool, tonight, your number two favorite. Besides, if Wong Hu finds out you were here and you didn't eat it, he'll throw another of his Chinese tantrums and maybe threaten to quit again!"

"All right, I'll have it!"

"Ha! I knew that would get you. My mother says pastafazoo is the Italian version of chicken soup. I think you could use some comfort food."

Boyd endured a couple torturous nights, anticipating seeing Noreen. Not helped by not hearing from Rachel. He picked up the phone several times and put it back down. It's proper for her to call me. There must be a good reason why she didn't. In a way I'm glad, my mind is distracted by Wednesday evening's meeting with Noreen.

There was a job that was ready to be started but he wasn't motivated and instead, busied himself staying in his barn home, writing up estimates, and doing some work on his bedroom and bathroom.

Wednesday evening as he was nervously getting ready to go to McGillicudy's, the phone rang. It was Rachel.

"Michael, the reason why you haven't heard from me," she paused, "I'll be leaving for Israel in a few days to meet with my son. He went there on a whim and desperately wants me to be with him and our relatives. He's never been there. It was a short notice and I'll be busy packing, preparing the necessary documents. I'm sorry but we won't have time to get together before I leave."

"I understand," Boyd said softly. He was a little put out, thinking, if she really wanted, we could get together briefly. But it leaves me in the right state of mind for my reunion with Noreen.

He walked through the door of McGillicudy's, stopped and looked around. Juny was behind the bar wiping glasses. When he saw Boyd he shook his head, meaning Noreen hadn't yet arrived. Boyd sat on a stool at the near end of the bar. Juny began to draw a draft for him.

"Not tonight Juny. I want to be in full control of my senses." Juny tossed out the beer and replaced it with a cola. Boyd sat quietly. Juny, uncharacteristically, didn't try to strike up a conversation.

Boyd looked around the restaurant imagining Noreen as she was the last time he saw her: dressed in a green, Celtic-style waitress' outfit, flitting quickly around the tables serving, smiling, putting off flirtatious men, answering questions from diners who sometimes only asked in order to hear her melodic Gaelic accent, giving off witty old-country sayings, her head tossing, shaking out her strawberry-blond curls.

He wondered – and worried – about how he'd feel when he'd first see her.

A rush of cold air came into the restaurant. Boyd turned and looked toward the door. Noreen stepped inside. She was dressed in a long black cloth coat that went down to mid-calf, revealing, black, high-heeled leather boots. A collar of gray fur was tightly closed around her neck. She didn't look like the Noreen he remembered. The girl who loved color in her clothes, green in particular.

Boyd's first thought was she looked taller then he remembered. He stood up and walked slowly to her as if not knowing how they would greet one another.

"Hello, Boyd," she said with a small, uneasy smile as she removed gray leather gloves.

As he approached her, he noticed her freckled-faced complexion had on make-up that hid them. He'd never seen her wearing anything other than lipstick and rouge. Her eyebrows were accented and arched. Her strawberry-blond hair was shorter, darker, less curly and tamed. Different, he thought, but still as beautiful as ever.

"Hi…Noreen," was the best he could do… and in a chocked voice.

She offered him a cheek to kiss and they hugged briefly, then pushed away, holding hands and looked each other over.

"Good to see you again, Michael. How have you been?" He noticed her voice sounded huskier, and there was no trace of the Irish brogue!

"Great to see you too, Noreen," "You look more beautiful than ever. And you've lost your Irish accent!" Boyd leaned back, tilting his head up and down to make it obvious he was looking her over. "You look so…New York City."

"Thank you," she said, beaming. "I finally decided to leave the Irish colleen…and the accent, back in Ireland…where they belong. It took some doing, taking classes and such."

"It'll take a little getting used to. But I like it. Let's find a table. I want to hear what you've been …up to. Obviously, quite a bit."

Noreen gave Juny a wave as Boyd led her over to a table…the same table where he and Rachel had sat. He suddenly made an abrupt change in direction and headed to another table. Noreen gave him a quizzical look.

"Let me take your coat." He folded her coat and placed it over the back of an empty chair. A few of the regular diners looked on and whispered, obviously recognizing the former, popular waitress.

She was wearing a blue knit dress with a low neckline, revealing a gold locket hanging from a gold chain. A wide, black leather belt and buckle matched the black, leather boots. As he folded the coat over the chair, he thought he would have preferred the old Noreen…brogue and all.

"What is it with the table selection, Boyd?" Noreen asked with an arched eyebrow, as they sat opposite each other.

"That other table rocks. I want to hear about you. I understand you've been in New York. For almost a year now." His mind was finally settling in, allowing him to come up with his typical, quips style. "Nice of you to stop by. And what have you been doing lately?" He was about to add; 'and why haven't you called me', but thought that was best, left for later, or when she offered it.

"Where do I start?" she said with a sigh. She paused, running her fingers through her hair, looking at him. "You're staring at me, Boyd."

"It's just that I'm amazed at the changes in you."

"You don't approve?"

"Quite the opposite."

"I'm glad. It took a lot of effort to bring them about." She paused, looking off. "I wasn't happy back in Ireland. America, you, this place, had spoiled…changed me forever." Looking reflective for a few moments: "I've become an American citizen, worked to get rid of the accent. I took courses at NYU to get my State teaching certification. I'm teaching in a private, pre-school facility for now, working part-time at Bloomingdale's and doing some presenter-modeling in trade shows at the convention center."

"Is there a significant other," Boyd boldly asked, but quickly thought he shouldn't have.

"How could I possibly find the time? I work, study, live in a tiny room in the Barbizon Hotel For Ladies to save money to finance my education. It's all I have time for."

"I applaud you for becoming so independent."

"Independent? I guess so. But I don't feel that way."

"Now that you're up-to-date with me, what have *you* been doing?" she asked with a squint and a raised eyebrow. "Besides checking out the tables that rock?"

"I see your sense of humor hasn't changed," he said with a wry smile. "I've been working of course, camping up in the Adirondack property, fishing, hunting, finishing the barn. All much the same as before. I too haven't had time for much else."

"Oh, that wonderful barn, I really missed it."

"The barn? How about me? Evidently I wasn't missed since you never bothered to call or anything."

"Boyd, I didn't want any distractions. I set goals for myself. I'm not there yet but I feel I'm on the right track now."

Juny came over to the table. "Don't mean to break up the happy reunion, but would you care to give me your order?" said Juny. "We do have expenses to pay here ya know."

"Same old Juny," Noreen giggled.

"Yeah, he's still a bundle of laughs," says Boyd

in mock derision.

"And why haven't you fixed that table's leg, Mr. McGillicudy?" asked Noreen nodding to the other table.

Juny's brow knit. "Table leg?" The experienced barkeep quickly knew to give the right answer. "Oh yes, that. I forgot."

After they placed their food and drink order, they stared quietly at each other. Is it possible, thought Boyd, we've run out of things to say so soon? After not seeing or hearing from each other for almost two years? He decided to get right to the point.

"Is there anything left of our relationship, Noreen?"

She looked at him surprised that he had such intentions. "That's a difficult question, Boyd," Noreen answered softly.

Boyd once again felt it was something he shouldn't have asked.

She seemed hard put for an answer. "A few embers…maybe," said Noreen indifferently.

"Well embers *can* be fanned back to life."

"Only if you want them to. But, is it really what you want, Boyd? Or are you only trying to massage your ego?" Noreen said challengingly. "Relationships have to lead somewhere. You never gave any thought to anything…permanent all the time we were together." She stopped. "Oh, I'm sorry. I shouldn't have said that. My own attitude wasn't perfect either and was more about my disappointment with my teaching career not going anyplace."

Juny brought over their drinks suspending the uncomfortable moment. "Your dinner will be here in a few minutes."

"Still the fastest service in town," said Noreen. "I guess the old Chinese, wonder-chef is still at the helm."

"Oh, he sure is," Juny assured. "He'll be out to say hello after his kitchen duties are finished. He insists the dinner is on him. Hmph! He's been here so long he thinks he owns the place."

Conversation during their dinner was centered on Noreen's questions about their mutual friends, marriages, newborns and changes in the town.

They had after dinner drinks at the bar with Juny regaling them with stories about the different and unusual customers of the restaurant.

"Some things never change," said Noreen as she put her hand on Juny's arm, while laughing at his tales. "And I love that they don't." She paused. "I feel like I'm back … home again."

The evening ended when Noreen stood up and asked for her coat. Boyd was disappointed, feeling he wanted to be with her the whole night.

"I'm a working girl, you know."

He walked her out to a waiting taxi, "When will I see you again?"

"I…I really don't know when, Boyd. I really am so busy."

"Busy or not, you have to eat! I could meet

you for dinner…in the city. Give me your phone number and I'll give you a call."

"The only phone is the pay phone in the hall. It's hard to get messages. "I'll call you."

"Sounds to me like the old, 'don't call me, I'll call you, bit.'"

Noreen chuckled. "You're as silly as ever," she said as she entered the cab.

As it started to pull away, Boyd waved, she returned the wave with the broadest smile he had seen the whole evening.

He went back inside and sat at the bar.

Juny came over and leaned on the bar. "Boyd, ya look like a man with problems." He grinned, "The kind of problems other men would envy. Give me your thoughts then I'll tell ya what I think."

"It's pretty obvious I'm torn between…I think I'm in love with two women. I haven't a clue which one I'd rather be with." He hesitated. "I don't want to play games with them like some other guys do."

Juny was staring at him, waiting.

"Noreen may make the choice for me. I might never hear from her again. She's not the predictable Noreen I once knew." He looked off in an ethereal way.

"Okay, Boyd, now, do ya wanna hear what I think?"

Taken out of his reverie, he shot back. "Of course! Don't I always?"

"Noreen's a known quantity. Ya have a history together. You're more the same kind of people. Rachel is different people. Would you go live in

Israel, if she wanted? I can answer that one for you because you'd made it clear a long time ago. You wouldn't even go to live in Ireland if that's what it took to—"

"I don't know what, or who, I want right now."

"Stop kidding yourself, Boyd!"

"I've got to think things through." Boyd got up. "Talk to you soon, Juny, Thanks for the dinner treat." As he walked away, Juny eyes followed him, shaking his head.

When he got up the next morning he was in a bad mood. Reluctantly, he picked up his phone messages. One was from David Sarnoff saying he should put the garage remote through the mail slot in the front door. He said he had mailed him the final payment and would get in touch soon about remodeling the unfinished part of the basement. He wished him and Rachel the best of luck. Which made Boyd feel guilty since he wasn't sure they would be a couple.

Boyd buried himself in a couple of jobs. His heart just wasn't in his work. It was taking him more time to get things done. He was annoyed at himself for letting his personal life get in the way of his work.

Late one evening he got an overseas phone call from Rachel. The connection was so bad he couldn't make out anything she was saying and she seemed to be in a rush. All he could make out was her saying, she would write him. A short letter followed. They were dated before Rachel had made the telephone call. She said she was looking into several universities for her son who had decided to make Israel his home. That was it.

Two weeks passed and there was no phone call from Noreen.

On a Saturday morning there was another letter in the mailbox from Rachel. He tore the letter open and read it as he walked back to the barn.

> *Dearest Michael,*
> *Sorry it's taken so long for me to write. My son Aaron is keeping me quite busy, especially since he has made up his mind to remain here in Israel. We've been examining universities and looking at dormitories and apartments.*
> *Michael, I hope you can understand what I'm going to say. I am going to remain here and make Israel my home again. It's where my roots are, where my family is, where I belong. I don't believe you would want to make your life here.*
> *I thank you for taking me out of my shell and showing me I'm capable of love, once again. I will*

miss you very much. Please do not try to dissuade me. I have made my decision and have many things to work out.
I will never forget you.
Rachel.

Boyd was stunned; his hands shook. She…she dumped me! But I realized it was a difficult decision for her. It must have taken a lot for her to make it. She really cared for me, I know it. It just wasn't meant to be.

"Well, McGillicudy, in an indirect way, you were right. Imagine! Rachel wrote me a 'Dear John'…my first. Here, read it."

When Juny finished it, Boyd asked him what he thought.

"Well m'boy," said Juny with sarcastic overtones, "it seems to me, if you were willing to move to Israel—"

"Of course, I'm not!"

"Get ready for another blow. There's no sense in holding it from you."

"It's about Noreen, isn't it?"

"Afraid so. She called and spoke to Maria yesterday. Told her that she wants to make the city her permanent home."

"My God, I got dumped twice in one day! What am I doing wrong, Juny?"

"Forget about that for now…it would take to long. What's important, she didn't close the door completely, like—. But I think you'd hafta move to the city if you want to hold on to her."

"Me? Live in New York City?"

"A beauty like her isn't going to be around forever, ya know. Heck, moving to the city is nowhere as hard as moving to Ireland…or Israel." Juny's face moved in close to Boyd'. He looked at the disheartened Boyd through squinted eyes. "She's changed and now if you want her, it's your turn to make changes…make your move!" He paused. "I can tell ya in one word, what it is you're doing wrong, my friend."

"In a word? Oh, come on! One word?"

"Commitment!" Juny replied. "Fear of commitment, my friend."

Boyd received a message from Sarnoff saying he'd like him to begin the improvements to his basement. Boyd apologized and told him he had several jobs going and would have to recommend another contractor.

"I understand, my friend, I very much understand," said Sarnoff."

Six months later.

Michael Thomas Boyd and Noreen Patricia Fitzgerald had been married in St. Paul's Roman Catholic Church in Landrock County. The reception took place at McGillicudy's Restaurant.

Noreen was teaching in the New York City School System. Boyd worked as a construction superintendent for a major New York City developer. He was enrolled in the Columbia University Evening School of Architecture. They purchased an apartment on the city's West side overlooking Central Park. Sunday dinners were often at the newly renamed, McGillicuddy's Ristorante Italiano, with overnight stays in the barn. Long holiday weekends and vacations were spent in the trailer on the Adirondack property.

THE END

COMMITMENT

Other Works by the Author

Out of Hong Kong

The exotic Far East city of the 1960's capitavates a young American naval officer. He accidentlly find himself in an upscale brothel and is put with a beautiful virgin. He attempts to save her from a life of prostitution. Each visit to Hong Kong presents a life altering experience. He adopts a waif girl, meets a mysterious courtesan, a stunning British divorcee. Years later, by chance, he finally finds the prostitute he tried to save.

No-Name Island

Post World War II, a six-man Navy detachement is sent on a highly classified mission to map a remote uninhabited tropical island where they find a leper colony manned by a musterious medical staff. Also, a hidden encampment of men and women, survivors of an accidentally sunk Japenese hospital ship, wh are not aware the war is ove. Unlikely scenarios for romance? Not quite.

Forever is Tomorrow

World War II calls Joel Silver to fight in the skies over North Africa. He ad his Luftwaffe adversary find themselves stranded in the Sahara Desert, The German dies. Joel survives. Circumstances force him to live out both lives with the love of two women.

Bavarian Girls

There were six. They were inseparable. Completing high school in Munich, they felt they could find a better life in America. All it took was getting there and finding the right American husband. Soon each was on her own path and they lost touch, Forty years later, in a Connecticut mansion, they came together once again in an unpredictable, more exciting reunion that they ever could have imagined.

Vince D'Angelo

Acknowledgments

Special thanks to Joanne Simon Tailele
with Simon Publishing LLC for her assistance
in formatting and printing this book.

www.SimonPublishingLLC.com